· O N E ·
SATURDAY
AFTERNOON

BY Barbara Baker · PICTURES BY Kate Duke

Dutton Children's Books · New York

Library of Congress Cataloging-in-Publication Data
Baker, Barbara, date.
One Saturday afternoon / by Barbara Baker; pictures by Kate Duke.
—1st ed.   p. cm.
Summary: Members of a bear family have a busy day
baking bread, making pictures, eating crayons, and eating the bread.
ISBN 0-525-45882-4 (hc)
[1. Family life—Fiction. 2. Bears—Fiction.] I. Duke, Kate, ill. II. Title.
PZ7.B1692201   1999   [E]—dc21   98-41605   CIP   AC

Published in the United States 1999 by Dutton Children's Books,
a division of Penguin Putnam Books for Young Readers
345 Hudson Street, New York, New York 10014
http://www.penguinputnam.com/yreaders/index.htm

Printed in Hong Kong
First Edition
1 3 5 7 9 10 8 6 4 2

For Michael and Susanna Naum
B.A.B.

For the bears of Washington Square, apt. 14E
K.D.

CONTENTS

MAMA

One Saturday afternoon

Mama wanted to go for a walk.

"I want to come, too," said Lily.

"Wait for me," said Rose.

"I need my carriage," said Daisy.

"Me, me, me," said Jack.

They all ran to Mama.

But Mama said,

"No."

"No?" said Papa.

"No," said Mama.

"I need to be alone."

Lily and Rose and Daisy and Jack began to cry.

"Oh dear," said Mama.

So Papa said,

"Who wants to help me make bread?"

Lily and Rose and Daisy and Jack

all ran to the kitchen.

"Thank you," said Mama to Papa.

Then Mama went out.

She went for a long walk. Alone.

Mama smelled the grass and flowers.

She felt the sun and the wind.

She saw some birds fly past.

She was happy.

Then Mama walked home.

She opened the door.

Something smelled wonderful.

Lily and Rose and Daisy and Jack
came running.

"We made bread," said Lily.

"Papa helped us," said Rose.

"It's in the oven," said Daisy.

"Up, up, up," said Jack.

Mama sat down.

Lily and Rose and Daisy and Jack

sat on Mama's lap.

"Did you have a good walk?" said Papa.

"Yes," said Mama. "I did.

And now it is *very* good

to be back home."

Lily was reading a book.

It had a lot of words.

It had a lot of pictures.

It was a good book.

Lily was happy.

"Play with me, Lily," said Rose.

"Not now," said Lily. "I am reading."

Daisy came over.

"I want to play, too," she said.

15

"I am not playing," said Lily.

"I am reading."

"Me," said Jack.

He tried to sit on Lily's lap.

He tried to take her book.

"I give up," said Lily.

"I will play with you.

We will play school."

Lily made Rose and Daisy and Jack

sit down.

"This is the school," she said.

"And *I* am the teacher.

You are the children in my class."

Lily got paper and crayons.

"Now, children," she said,

"it is time to do your work."

She gave the paper and crayons

to Rose and Daisy and Jack.

"You have to make a lot

of pictures," she said.

Rose and Daisy and Jack

got started.

Then Lily opened her book.

She began to read.

Lily was happy.

ROSE

"I want to be the teacher now,"

said Rose.

But no one listened.

Lily was reading her book.

Daisy was making a picture.

And Jack was eating a crayon.

"I want to be the teacher now,"

said Rose again.

"Shhh," said Lily. "I am busy."

"Shhh," said Daisy. "I am busy."

"Mmmm," said Jack. He was busy, too.

So Rose went to find Mama and Papa.

They were in the kitchen.

"I want to be the teacher now,"

said Rose.

"That's nice," said Papa.

He was cutting carrots.

"That's nice," said Mama.

She was cutting potatoes.

"No," said Rose.

"It is *not* nice.

"Lily and Daisy and Jack

will not listen to me.

They will not let me

be the teacher."

Rose began to cry.

DAISY

Daisy worked on her picture

for a long time.

She made a tree and a house

and a cat and a flower.

"Look, Lily," she said.

"I made a pretty picture."

Lily looked at the picture.

She took a crayon.

"Let me help you," she said.

"No!" cried Daisy.

She took her picture

to the kitchen.

"Look, Rose," she said.

"I made a pretty picture."

Rose looked at the picture.

"It is scribble-scrabble," she said.

"It is *not*," cried Daisy.

She took her picture

to Papa and Mama.

"Look at my picture," she said.

"Beautiful," said Papa.

"It is just what we needed," said Mama.

Then Mama got some tape.

She put the picture up

on the wall.

"It looks good there," said Mama.

"Just like a picture in a museum."

"Yes," said Daisy.

Then Daisy got her baby doll.

"We are not playing school anymore,"

she told her.

"We are going to a museum

to see a beautiful picture."

JACK

Jack was very busy.

First he made a picture

on his paper.

Then he ate part of a red crayon.

Then he made a picture

on the wall.

Lily looked up from her book.

"Jack!" she cried.

"Give that crayon to me."

"No," said Jack.

He put the crayon into his mouth.

"Spit it out," said Lily.

"No," said Jack.

So Lily went to tell Mama.

Jack took the red crayon

out of his mouth.

Lily came back with Mama.

"Look at the wall," said Lily.

"Look what he did!"

"Oh, dear," said Mama.

"He is a bad boy," said Lily.

"He is just a baby," said Mama.

Then Mama picked Jack up.

"Time for your nap, Jack," she said.

"*No!*" cried Jack.

Mama took Jack to his crib.

She put him in.

"Have a nice nap," she said.

"*No!*" said Jack.

Mama left.

"No, no, no," said Jack.

Then he was quiet.

Jack still had the red crayon.

Jack was very busy.

PAPA

The kitchen smelled wonderful.

Vegetable stew was cooking

in a big pot.

Warm bread was cooling

on the table.

"I have worked hard all day,"

said Papa.

"Now I will have some bread."

Papa cut a piece of warm fresh bread.

He sat down.

"This bread needs butter,"

said Papa.

"Then it will be just right."

He went to get the butter.

When he came back,

the piece of bread was gone.

"Yummy," said Rose.

"That was *my* bread," said Papa.

He cut himself another piece of bread.

He put butter on it.

He sat down.

"This bread and butter needs jam,"

said Papa.

"Then it will be just right."

He went to get the jam.

When he came back,

the piece of bread was gone.

"Yummy," said Daisy.

"That was *my* bread," said Papa.

He cut himself another piece of bread.

He put butter and jam on it.

He sat down.

"This bread and butter and jam needs

a glass of milk," said Papa.

"Then it will be just right."

He went to get some milk.

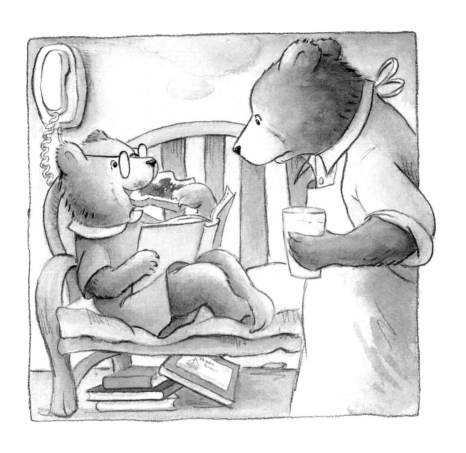

When he came back,

the piece of bread was gone.

"Yummy," said Lily.

"That was *my* bread," said Papa.

Mama came into the kitchen.

She was holding Jack.

"Who is eating bread?" said Mama.

"That bread is for dinner."

"*I* did not have any," said Papa.

He looked at Rose and Daisy and Lily.

"Me, me, me," said Jack.

"Oh, well," said Mama.

She cut some bread for Jack.

She cut some bread for herself.

She cut some more bread for Lily
and Rose and Daisy.

Then she cut a big piece for Papa.

"Thank you," said Papa.

Then Papa put butter and jam

on the bread.

He drank some cold milk.

He sat down.

He took a big bite of bread.

"Yummy," said Papa. "Just right."

3-8/00